Spellbound

Adapted by Beth Beechwood

Based on the series created by Todd J. Greenwald

Part One is based on the episode, "Alex's Choice," Written by Matt Goldman

Part Two is based on the episode, "New Employee," Written by Peter Murrieta

DISNEP PRESS

New York

Printed in the United States of America

First Edition
1 3 5 7 9 10 8 6 4 2

Library of Congress Catalog Card Number: 2008925120
ISBN 978-1-4231-1605-9

For more Disney Press fun, visit www.disneybooks.com
Visit DisneyChannel.com

PART ONE

Chapter One

Alex Russo and Harper Evans were walking through the hallway on the way to their lockers. They'd just finished a history test that had been much more difficult than either of them had expected. Sometimes, no matter how hard they studied, all those dates got confusing.

"Whoa," Harper said to Alex. "That last multiple-choice question was really hard. I got A."

Alex shook her head. "I got D," she said.

"And I'm pretty sure I'm right."

"D wasn't even close," Harper replied, a puzzled expression on her face. "Why are you so sure you're right?"

"No, I got a D on the test," Alex said with a smile. "I'm sure I'm right about that." Alex wasn't exactly a great student. She was good at other things, like shopping and magic. That would have to do for now.

Just then, Alex spotted Gigi Hollingsworth coming down the hall. The girls had been rivals since kindergarten. Alex couldn't stand the way Gigi reigned over everyone else like she was just so important. "Oh, look," she said to Harper, "Gigi's handing out invitations to her annual tea."

"I'm so glad we're not invited," Harper said rolling her eyes. "Then we'd have to talk like this." Speaking in a pseudo-British accent she continued, "Hello, Mumsy. Hello, Popsy. Isn't this a lovely tea? Do you think my pinkie's high enough?" She lifted her pinkie finger up from her soda can, pretending she was holding a china teacup.

"No, higher," Alex encouraged her, also putting on a British accent, "like this." She lifted her pinkie as high as it could possibly go and pointed her nose straight up in the air. "Because if you're going to a fancy tea, you need to act like you've smelled something terrible." She sniffed and then cringed, pretending to smell something unpleasant.

Alex and Harper giggled uncontrollably until they noticed someone standing beside them. It was none other than the queen snob herself, Gigi.

"Good afternoon, Alex. Harper. How is this lovely day treating you so far?" Gigi said with a huge smile. Gigi had very long blond hair that was styled to perfection, and she always wore the trendiest clothes. She also had a group of snobby friends who followed her wherever she went. But today her friends weren't looking so hot. Their faces were puffy and swollen with welts.

Alex ignored Gigi and turned to her rival's friends. "What happened to your faces? Apply your makeup with a hammer?"

"That is really funny, Alex, but incorrect," one of the girls responded.

"What you see is the result of a new method where they inject stuff into your forehead," the other girl explained. "Then, in a few days, it falls down into your cheekbones."

Alex stared at the girls in shock. Normally, Gigi and her friends were ready to make fun of Alex and Harper at a moment's notice.

"Wait a minute," Alex said. "Time-out. Why aren't you fighting back? We just bagged on your faces—which should be in a bag."

Gigi and her wannabe friends just laughed. Alex couldn't believe it.

"See?" Alex said. "I did it again. Why aren't

you insulting me? Remember? We don't like each other." How could they have forgotten, Alex wondered. They'd had a mutual distaste for each other since elementary school.

Gigi simply clicked her tongue. "Oh, but that was back when we were young and foolish."

"That was yesterday," Alex reminded them. She knew something was up, but she couldn't figure out what it was.

"My point exactly," Gigi replied. She waved her hand as though that would erase the years of pranks and mean comments. "That's why I'm inviting you both to my tea this weekend."

At this, Harper lit up. "Your tea? I've always wanted to go. Thanks, Gigi, this is great." Harper was genuinely ecstatic. Alex was floored by her friend's reaction. What Alex didn't realize was that Harper had longed for an invitation from such an exclusive group.

Harper knew Alex would never be able to relate to such a thing. Alex was funny and well liked and didn't need to impress anyone into being her friend.

"What?" Alex asked, turning to Harper. But Harper didn't notice her at all. She was still staring at Gigi excitedly.

"Well, I hope you guys can make it," Gigi said. "Come, girls. Let's go make fun of Eddie until he cries." She started walking away, and the girls fell into line behind her.

Harper turned to Alex. She knew it was finally time to come clean to her best friend, even though Alex wouldn't approve at all. "Alex, I've always wanted to go to a high tea!" Harper exclaimed. "I love the idea of eating tiny sandwiches."

"You're serious?" Alex asked, utterly puzzled by her friend's abrupt turnaround. She couldn't believe that one invitiation could make Harper forget all the mean things Gigi had done in the past. "I don't mean to sound unsupportive, but are you out of your mind, woman? Gigi has terrorized us since we were in kindergarten."

"Well," Harper said, "I think Gigi's taking the high road. And I want to reach out to her. If you want to be a Negative Nellie, then go ahead." Harper didn't know what else to say. She really wanted to go to the tea, and Alex would just have to be okay with that.

"Okay, the only Nellie I know is Nellie Rodriguez," Alex replied, trying to make a joke. "And she's a very positive, upbeat person."

Just then, as if on cue, Nellie Rodriguez came down the hall toward them.

"Hi, Nellie. You going to Gigi's tea?" Harper asked.

"Yeah!" Nellie said, beaming. "I can't wait! It's going to be so much fun!" Then she and Harper hurried off to their next class, excitedly talking over the details of the tea.

"So, what are you going to wear?" Harper asked Nellie.

Alex was left on her own as they walked away, and she was beyond annoyed. She couldn't understand how anyone would want to go to Gigi's tea. "Ugh," she muttered as she trudged into her next class. "There's nothing worse than a Positive Nellie." She couldn't believe that all this time, Harper had wanted to be part of Gigi's circle of friends. Alex felt as if she didn't know her friend at all. And that made her feel terrible.

Chapter Two

After school that day, Alex's brothers, Max and Justin, were already bickering as they pushed through the door of the Waverly Sub Station, their family's restaurant. Their mom, Theresa Russo, was trying to do some work behind the counter. She was in charge of both the family and the restaurant while Jerry Russo was away on business for a few days.

"I can't believe you won't let me go into the

lair. You're bunk," Max said to Justin as they approached the counter.

"I'm not the one who said you can't go in the lair," Justin tried to explain. "Dad said no one can while he's out of town. Call me bunk." He shook his head. His little brother could be so annoying.

While he was gone, Mr. Russo had left strict instructions that none of the kids be allowed into the wizard lair. Alex, Justin, and Max were wizards-in-training. Their father, a former wizard himself, knew the trouble a young wizard could get into before knowing the ins and outs of all the spells he or she could cast.

To prevent any magical mishaps, he taught wizard lessons every Tuesday and Thursday, and gave homework assignments in between. He knew the kids were disappointed about missing lessons while he was away. But he didn't want his wife, a mortal, to have to contend with magic gone awry. Mrs. Russo was thankful for that reprieve since she was already feeling overwhelmed with the restaurant. The bank deposit was due in a matter of hours and she was not even close to being ready.

"Then how am I supposed to study these new pocket spell books that Dad's going to quiz us on when he gets home?" Max asked. He shook the small book that was in his hand in his older brother's face.

At that moment, Mrs. Russo stepped in. She had been listening as she worked, and the whole conversation was getting on her nerves. "You'll study like you do for regular school," she said to both boys. "You'll sit here and do your work, and I'll do mine. With your dad gone for the weekend, I promised I'd do the bank deposit."

"I can't believe Dad's making us memorize twenty spells," Justin whined. "It's like he's gone, but he's not gone."

Mrs. Russo just shrugged and went back

to her work. Justin turned his attention to his own spell book. He was disappointed that the wizard lessons their father taught were on hold until Mr. Russo returned. Justin much preferred *using* magic as opposed to simply reading about it. But he also understood that if he wanted to be the best wizard in the family, he'd have to put in some study time.

Max was working hard, too. He sat on a stool in front of the counter and focused on the spells he was reading. As his concentration grew, he started bouncing his leg on the stool. Then he started shaking his leg uncontrollably and making grunting and sniffing noises.

Justin glanced over at his brother. He stared for a moment, but Max didn't seem to notice him at all. Finally, Justin sighed and said, "Can you at least stop shaking your leg? I'm trying to concentrate."

"Oh, shaking my leg is how I concentrate,"

Max explained, still not looking up from his book.

But Justin couldn't take it. His little brother was driving him crazy! He flicked Max's ear to try and get him to stop.

"Cut it out!" Max yelled.

"That's how *I* concentrate," Justin explained.

The whole scene was driving Mrs. Russo crazy. "Guys! Please, I'm trying to do this deposit."

"I know. Isn't Max so annoying?" Justin asked, trying to get his mother to take his side.

"You're the one who flicked my ear," Max said.

"Oh, you mean like this?" Justin asked, flicking his brother's ear again. The two of them went at it then, flicking and pushing each other until Mrs. Russo had had quite enough.

"Okay, that's it," she said loudly. "That's it! Come on. You guys are going to study your magic in the lair." The boys looked at each other but stayed put. "Come on," she said again, already halfway into the kitchen.

Justin and Max scrambled off their stools and followed her through the kitchen. They stopped in front of the door to the lair. There was a giant lock on it.

"See?" Justin said. "We can't even get in if we want. Dad put a lock on it. There's probably some kind of complicated magical spell on the lock that we'll never be able to break."

Mrs. Russo glanced over at the wall adjacent to the lair. There was a big key hanging on a hook. She smirked. "Or a giant key hanging on a hook right here." So maybe she wasn't a wizard, she thought. But she wasn't useless!

Max was stunned. "I thought that was a decoration," he said.

Mrs. Russo unlocked the door. "Come on," she told her sons. "Get in the lair. And don't tell your dad I let you in there." She closed the door behind them. For a minute, she contemplated locking them in and then thought better of it. No, she said to herself as she set the lock down on the counter. As tempting as it was, she had to let them out again.

Alex walked into the kitchen as Mrs. Russo turned around. The whole way home from school she had tried to understand why Harper would want to be Gigi's friend, but she couldn't and she was still really upset.

"You know what today is a great day for?" Alex asked her mother. But before Mrs. Russo could answer, Alex continued, "Today is a great day for throwing myself into work. Take orders and not talk about my problems, slice salami and not talk about my problems, be nice to rude customers and not tell them about my problems. You know me, service with a smile."

Mrs. Russo noted the sarcasm oozing from Alex's voice and knew what that meant. Alex needed to vent. "Oh, honey. You sound like you want to talk about your problems," she said.

"Mom, why are you always in my business?"

"Okay, fine," Mrs. Russo said, holding up her hands defensively. She turned around, about to head back out to the counter to do her work.

"All right, I'll tell you," Alex said with a sigh. "Gigi invited Harper and I to her tea, but Harper's going to go. She thinks Gigi's nice all of a sudden." Even as she said it, Alex couldn't believe it. How could Harper do this?

"Well, people change," Mrs. Russo offered. "Maybe Gigi *is* nicer."

"Mom, if I'm going to tell you about my problems, you have to agree with them," Alex explained.

"Okay, okay," her mother said. Now fully on board, she shook her head and continued, "Gigi. Horrible. Mean."

"I know," Alex agreed enthusiastically. "Isn't she? But Harper doesn't think so. So I guess Harper and I aren't friends anymore."

She hated to say this. But the truth was, Alex could never be friends with someone who was friends with Gigi. She just couldn't! Gigi was mean and shallow and made fun of people she didn't even know that well—Harper and Alex included.

"Oh, don't say that," Mrs. Russo said. "You and Harper have been friends forever. And you'll always be friends. You'll just have your ups and your downs."

"Right. Like when we were nine, and we had the lemonade stand, and Harper kept all the money," Alex said remembering one of their past disagreements.

"Well, she did do all the work," Mrs. Russo reminded her daughter.

"Mom!" Alex yelled. Her mother had clearly forgotten the rules of their little talk.

"Sorry," Mrs. Russo said with a shrug.

Chapter Three

Down in the wizard lair, Justin and Max were still at it. Max was driving Justin crazy with his throat-clearing noises and leg-bouncing. "Where's the spell to get you to stop shaking your leg?" Justin demanded, glaring at his brother. Before Max could respond, something came flying out of one of the cubbies on the light wall, distracting the boys from their bickering.

"Wizard mail," Max said. He got up from

his seat to retrieve the canister. "You know, we always get wizard mail, but we've never sent any out."

"You're right," Justin said. Then he got an idea. "Let's send out some prank mail." He grabbed a pencil and pad and cleared his throat. "Uh," he thought hard about what to put in the note. "Stranded on a deserted island in . . . in . . . the Lava Sea!"

Max looked at his older brother with a puzzled look on his face. "There's a Lava Sea?" he asked.

"I don't know. It's prank mail," Justin explained. He didn't care if his letter made any sense, he was just trying to have some fun. He didn't think there was any harm in that.

Max nodded, finally catching on to Justin's plan. And he knew just what to add to Justin's message. "Got it, got it. Wait," Max said excitedly. "All we have to eat is hot rocks."

"I like your thinking," Justin said as he wrote that down. When he finished, he rolled up the paper and stuck it in the clear glass mail bottle. He poised himself to throw the bottle back into the cubby in the wall. "And now," he said, getting into position, "*boop* . . . we send out our first piece of wizard mail." The mail was sucked back through the wall, whereupon Justin sang ominously, "*Dun-dun-dun-duh.*"

"Cool! Now what?" Max asked, sitting down at the table.

Justin sat beside his brother and exhaled loudly. "Now, we wait," he said tapping his fingers against each other.

Max laughed a little and rubbed his hands together. He liked this plan! He couldn't wait to see the response they'd get. "*Whoo!* Oh, now we're having fun, huh?" he said.

"This is awesome," Justin agreed.

They sat at the table waiting to see what would come of their first prank mail. But nothing was happening. Finally, after a couple of hours with no response, they gave up and headed back upstairs.

The next day at school, Harper came bounding down the stairs to find Gigi and her friends chatting together. Harper was glad she had run into them. Yesterday at this time, she and Gigi had been enemies. And today, she was one of the guests at Gigi's tea! She just knew it was going to be a great day.

"Hey," Harper said to them.

"Harper! Hi!" they shouted enthusiastically.

Harper was beside herself with glee.

Alex was standing at her locker watching the whole exchange when Harper came over. "Hey, Harper, what's up?" she asked her friend. She had made up her mind to be nice and try to be supportive, even if the thought of Harper being friends with those girls disgusted her.

"Oh, Gigi invited me to a sleepover," Harper gushed. "She wants me to make my little snickerdoodles. You know, the ones with the red-hot candies. Obviously, she really wants to be my friend. It's unbelievable."

"Yeah, it's unbelievable," Alex said, rolling her eyes. "As in, I don't believe it. I mean, come on. Have you seen anyone finish one of your spicy snickerdoodles? It's Gigi—she doesn't like us. If she invites you to her slumber party, it's just to put whipped cream in your hand while you're sleeping and then tickle your nose." Alex wished she hadn't had to say anything, but she was sure there was an ulterior motive for Gigi's behavior, and she didn't want Harper to get hurt.

Harper glared at Alex. "I thought you were going to be supportive," she said. Upset by Alex's response, Harper went back over to Gigi and her friends.

"I am!" Alex called after Harper. "I ate

24

your snickerdoodles the first time you made them!"

But Harper wasn't listening. She was already with her new friends, her gaze fixated on a sparkly, pink box Gigi was holding. "What's that?" she asked.

"It's the crown we're going to present the best newcomer at the tea," Gigi answered.

"Oh, can I see it?" Harper replied. She hadn't known a crown was being given out! She promised herself she'd go home that night and practice her decorum. If she could be crowned best newcomer, she'd be Gigi's friend as well as show Alex how wrong she was about Gigi's new attitude.

Gigi dismissed Harper's request with sugary sweetness. "Oh, no, no, silly. It's a surprise."

"I can't wait!" Harper said, giggling her way out the door and heading to her next class.

"Neither can we." Gigi smirked after Harper was gone. All of her friends laughed.

Alex had seen the whole thing. "Something's up," she said suspiciously. She pulled her spell book out of her locker and closed the door. Then she ducked into a corner and flipped through the book, looking for a spell. When she found the right one, she took a deep breath, exhaled, and said, "Some people are a gem. Some people are a rat. To learn who's who, give me the ear of a bat." And then, one of her ears turned into the ear of a bat, which might not have been very attractive, but it sure was useful.

"Oh, my gosh," one of Gigi's friends was saying. "Harper came so close to seeing the crown."

"I want to see it," the other girl said.

"Okay," Gigi said, laughing. She pulled out a shiny crown that had a big red *L* on it. "Do you see the *L*? It stands for 'loser.' And it's going to look so good on Harper when she's crowned the biggest loser."

"Yeah, at our 'Who Can Bring the Biggest Loser' party," another of the girls said. They all broke out in hysterics.

Alex was shocked. She had known Gigi was evil and that someone that mean couldn't change overnight. But she hadn't imagined Gigi could sink so low. Now Alex just had to find a way to convince her best friend that Gigi was only pretending to be nice so she could embarrass Harper at the party. It wasn't going to be easy. . . .

Chapter Four

After school that day, Justin and Max headed back down to the wizard lair. Their plan was to hang out and wait for a reply to their prank mail. They even managed to keep themselves entertained while they waited.

"What does this one smell like?" Justin asked Max, holding a bottle of elixir up to his brother's nose.

Max sniffed it and made a face. "The stuff

that grows between your toes," he said. Then he paused. "Mixed with a little earwax," he added.

Justin looked at the label. "Amazing!" he said. "You're right."

Suddenly, a bottle came shooting out from the wall and flew across the room.

"The bottle's back!" Justin shouted. They both ran over to retrieve it, but Justin got there first and opened it.

"What's it say?" Max asked.

Justin cleared his throat and began, "We have received your plea for help. Do not move or leave the island. The hot Lava Sea will burn you up."

Max shrugged. "Good to know," he said.

Justin continued, "Emergency wizards will arrive to rescue you soon."

"They bought it!" Max was elated. Their first prank had been a success!

But there was more. Justin was still reading.

"Please use the emergency supplies to stay alive until we arrive."

"What?" Max asked. "There aren't any emergency supplies. They're pranking us back!" This will be even more fun, Max thought. An ongoing prank with other wizards!

But Max and Justin quickly realized it wasn't a prank. Or at least, if it was, the other wizards were going all out. Because, suddenly, a life raft appeared and inflated right before their eyes.

"EMERGENCY WIZARD SUPPLIES," Justin said, reading the sign on the box inside the raft.

"Oh, a life raft," Max said. "I wonder if it's a magical life raft." He'd barely finished his thought when tons of crates and backpacks filled with more supplies suddenly appeared inside the raft as well. It was magical all right. "Wow." Max chuckled. "Emergency wizards are coming. They think we're really in trouble."

"Uh, Max," Justin said slowly. His little brother clearly didn't realize what had happened, and Justin had to try to find a way to explain the situation to him. "Emergency wizards are coming. We really *are* in trouble!"

Suddenly, Max understood: they were going to get caught playing a prank! "Well, maybe there's a chance they won't find us," he offered. But he knew that would be impossible when a red flashing light and siren started to go off. A giant neon sign appeared above them that read, SURVIVORS HERE. As if that weren't enough, the sign had an arrow pointing directly at Justin and Max.

This was not good.

Meanwhile, Alex was dealing with her own problems. After school, she had headed to the grocery store with Harper. When Harper was busy choosing an apple, Alex noticed something different about her friend's outfit.

"What are you wearing those gloves for?" Alex asked, looking at the white satin gloves covering Harper's hands.

"I'm getting used to them for Gigi's tea," Harper replied. "I need to practice handling things."

Alex couldn't get over the lengths Harper was going to for this tea—she hardly recognized her best friend.

"Why?" Alex asked just as Harper reached for an apple.

Harper selected a perfect, ripe red apple and tried to pick it up. But the slippery fabric made it hard for her to grab the apple. It spun out of her fingers and fell back into the pile, causing the rest of the apples in the bin to tumble forward. Dozens of apples fell to the ground.

"That's why," Harper said. She bent down and started to pick up the apples. When she realized Alex was just standing there beside her, she stood up and looked at her friend. "Aren't you going to help me?"

"Why?" Alex asked, confused. "They're already bruised." She waited, trying to figure out how to break her news to Harper. She had to find a way to keep her from going to Gigi's party. "Harper," Alex started with a sigh, "maybe you shouldn't go to Gigi's tea." She decided it was best to just be honest. "It's really a 'Who Can Bring the Biggest Loser' contest," she explained, bracing herself for Harper's reaction.

But Harper just scoffed at the party theme. "'Biggest Loser' contest? Alex, I can't believe you're making stuff up. It's just sad." Harper didn't believe that Gigi would do something like that, so she just brushed off Alex's news.

"I'm not making it up," Alex protested. "I heard Gigi say it."

"Oh, Alex," Harper said. "I know you wanted to hear that, but we all want to hear a lot of things we're never going to hear."

Alex wished Harper could see that what she'd said applied to her most of all. It was clear that Harper wanted to be accepted by Gigi and her friends, and Alex knew that was not going to happen.

"You're never going to believe me, are you?" Alex asked.

Harper clicked her tongue just like Gigi. "Alex, Alex, Alex," she said in a patronizing tone. "Real friends accept each other branching out. They don't get competitive and jealous and make up ridiculous stories."

"So, you're going to that tea no matter what I say?" Alex asked.

"Yes, I am," Harper said.

Alex sighed. She knew what she had to do. "I can't believe I'm doing this, but I'm going, too."

"Oh, my gosh!" Harper said, jumping up and down.

"Yep, you're my friend," Alex explained. "So I have to be with you through thick and thin. And I have a feeling that this tea is going to be thick. Or thin. Whichever one's bad," she finished, half-smiling. Going to the tea was the only way to protect Harper, and even if Alex couldn't do that, at least she'd be there to pick up the pieces when it was all over.

"Thank you, Alex. This is going to be awesome. We can support each other. I'll come over four hours before the tea for a pretea tea, and then we can get dressed together and practice our manners and—"

"How about I meet you there?" Alex interrupted, giving her friend a wry smile.

Chapter Five

With emergency wizards on the way, the last place Justin and Max wanted to be was in the lair. They darted upstairs to the apartment above the restaurant to talk to their mom. Maybe they could convince her to let them leave town for a little while.

They found Mrs. Russo in the kitchen preparing dinner. Justin cleared his throat to get her attention. "Hey, Mom, we were just wondering if maybe we could go to Grandma's."

"Oh?" Mrs. Russo asked, looking at the boys skeptically. "Why?"

"Why?" Max shouted. "Because we pulled a prank, and now emergency wizards are after us!"

"Look," Justin said, with a laugh, trying to make light of the situation. "It's not that bad. We just sent a prank message in a bottle through the wizard mail saying we needed help, and emergency wizards responded, saying they're coming." He was trying desperately to downplay the whole ordeal, but Mrs. Russo wasn't buying it. She gasped. "Okay, it's bad," Justin admitted.

"You guys are in an enormous amount of trouble," their mother told them.

"We know, we know," Max said. "We wish we never would've asked to go into the lair and you never would've let us in." He thought that if his mother felt some guilt herself then maybe she would help them out of their mess.

"Yep," Justin agreed. "It's really your fault."

He laughed nervously. But he knew his mother. She wouldn't let them take the fall for this whole thing.

Mrs. Russo thought for a minute and then said, "Well, maybe we can go stay at Grandma's."

That night, as Mrs. Russo and her sons planned their escape, Alex wondered how she and Harper would make it out of Gigi's tea as friends. She wished she could think up an excuse to get them both out of the whole thing. But if Harper wouldn't believe the truth, Alex would have an even harder time convincing her of a hastily made-up lie.

The next morning while her brothers were packing, Alex headed over to the hotel where Gigi's tea was being held. Once there, she spotted Harper right away—wearing her white gloves.

The hostess breezed into the room in a bright yellow dress covered by a lacy white apron. Her clothes fit the theme of a garden tea party, but her face was extremely serious. She stood at the front of the room and welcomed the girls with a less than enthusiastic tone. "Ladies, welcome to tea at The Hotel Fleur d'*Blaeglublafluflaaeghflaa*."

"The Hotel what?" Alex asked. "How do you spell that?" She had no idea what the woman had said.

"In French," the hostess answered Alex. Then she turned to the rest of the crowd and said, "We are proud to present this tea, served to you on the finest china imported from Japan. Hosted by young Miss Gigi Hollingsworth."

And then Gigi made her grand entrance. The wannabes all gasped when they saw her.

"I know you'll act in the most ladylike fashion. Enjoy your tea here at The Hotel Fleur d'*Blaeglublafluflaaeghflaa*," the hostess concluded. Then she exited the room with a flourish.

Though Harper's gaze was fixed on Gigi, along with everyone else's, Alex was still thinking about what the hostess had said. "Remind me to stop at the gift shop and get a T-shirt with the hotel's name on it," she said to Harper.

Harper didn't respond to Alex's comment, because no sooner had Alex uttered it than Gigi approached them. Harper was so excited she could hardly contain herself. She couldn't believe that she and Alex had finally been invited to Gigi's tea, and that they were actually there, all dressed up for the best day of Harper's life!

"Harper, Alex, I'm so glad you guys could make it," Gigi gushed. "I mean, your attendance is going to make this the most special tea I've ever had."

"Well, thanks, Gigi. I'm so glad you invited me," Harper said with a broad smile.

"Oh, not as glad as I am," Gigi said. Then

she tapped her teacup with a spoon and said, "Um, attention, everyone." The other guests joined in the tapping—even Alex tried to delicately make some noise on her cup, too. She figured that while she was there she might as well play along. Only, it didn't quite work out. As soon as her spoon touched the china, the cup shattered. The other girls turned and stared at Alex.

"Okay, then," Gigi said, alarmed at Alex's mishap. "Well, now that we've all had a chance to mingle, I have a huge announcement I'd like to make."

Alex really didn't want to wait around to hear this, and she especially didn't want Harper to hear it. It would kill her. She grabbed Harper's arm and whispered, "Let's go look at the ladies' room. I hear it's so fancy the toilet's filled with bottled water." She laughed nervously, hoping this would pique Harper's interest long enough for her to miss the announcement. "Plus, the soaps look like little seashells."

"Oh, I love those!" Harper exclaimed. "But I really should stay. I think Gigi's going to say something important. She usually does." Harper was mesmerized by Gigi, and Alex panicked. Apparently her description of the bathroom just wasn't enough to entice Harper away from her new "friend" and the awful speech she was about to make.

"And now it's time to announce the best newcomer and present her with the special crown," Gigi was saying.

Alex had to do something. And quickly, too.

"I really think we should go," she urged. "If we don't go soon, the soaps will get used and just be soapy lumps."

Harper was getting annoyed now. "Look, I don't care about your soapy lumps," she shot back at Alex. Then she again turned her full attention to Gigi and the big announcement.

"I can't let this happen," Alex mumbled, stepping back from the crowd. She had to act fast. She pulled her spell book from her purse. "Truth spell, truth spell . . ." she said, flipping through the book. Finally, she found what she was looking for. *Some are evil, some are kind. But now, all must speak their mind.*"

All of a sudden, one of Gigi's friends, who had been waiting enthusiastically for Gigi's announcement, spoke up before Gigi could continue. "If my parents could afford the same dermatologist as Gigi, I'd be way prettier than her." She slapped her hand to her mouth. "Oh, my gosh, did I just say that?"

Gigi's other good friend spoke up, too. "After I clean my ears, I look." She gasped in horror at what she'd just admitted. "What's wrong with me?" She started to hyperventilate.

Harper was the next one to blurt out a secret. "Please pick me for best newcomer! Please, please, oh, pretty please with a cherry on top." She covered her mouth with her gloved hand, embarrassed by her outburst.

Even Nellie, Positive Nellie, spoke the truth—and it wasn't exactly positive thinking. "I hope this isn't one of those loser teas. It'll be the fifth one I've been to this year." She gasped, too, and then laughed to cover it up.

Gigi looked around the room at her guests and said, "Jennifer looks way prettier than me. I'm going to talk her into a bad haircut. Hey, Jen! I'm going to talk you into a bad haircut! Why did I just say that?" She couldn't believe she'd actually said that out loud. This was not at all how this was supposed to go. She was supposed to be making a fool of someone else, not herself!

Alex was very pleased with her handiwork. "Oh, this is going better than I thought." But then, she turned to the crowd and said, "Hey, everybody, I'm a wizard!" She hadn't expected to get bitten by the truth bug, so she was as shocked as the crowd.

"Huh?" they all said, turning to stare at her once again.

Meanwhile, back at the Russos' apartment, panic was ensuing.

"You guys got everything?" Mrs. Russo said to the boys. "I called Grandma, and she's blowing up our mattresses." She looked at them then and her face became entirely serious. "So, when your dad gets back on Monday, we have to make sure we have our story straight." The boys nodded to indicate their agreement, and Mrs. Russo sighed. They were almost out of this mess!

Then she turned around to find two wizard police officers standing in front of her, blocking their exit. "Uh! Or we could get our story straight now," she said, her voice shaking.

One was tall, the other very short with

bushy eyebrows and sharp bottom teeth poking out of his mouth. "Officer Lamp," said the tall one, introducing himself. "This is my partner. He's a goblin."

The goblin officer was not happy with his introduction. "I have a name," he said to his partner.

"Yeah. But nobody can pronounce that," Officer Lamp replied, before turning his attention back to the Russos. "We're emergency wizards. I have a report here of someone using the wizard mail to request emergency services when, in fact, no services were required."

"Yeah, they pranked us," the goblin said, making a long story short.

"That's what I just said," Lamp protested.

"But you took too long, you know?" the goblin explained.

Mrs. Russo laughed, though it sounded strained. She was trying desperately to cover for her boys. "We're just an ordinary family enjoying the afternoon," she said lightly.

At the very same moment, both Justin and Max spoke up!

"You guys are in the wrong place, right?" Max said.

"What are you talking about?" Justin asked.

The Russos weren't doing a very good job of acting innocent.

The goblin looked at them skeptically. "This is the Russo family of Waverly Place, New York, New York? Home to wizards-in-training Justin, Alex, and Max?"

"These are not the droids you're looking for," Justin said, trying to confuse the wizards.

"What are you doing?" Officer Lamp asked. He sounded extremely annoyed.

"Nothing. I figured I'd give it a shot," Justin admitted sheepishly. He was getting his family into worse trouble by trying to get them out of it!

"Okay. I see," Officer Lamp said. Then he

turned to the goblin. "Was that short enough for you?"

"Oh, now we're doing short jokes?" the goblin retorted angrily. He was clearly a little insecure about his size.

"Guys," Max offered casually, "so, I guess we're cool, then?"

"Yeah. We're cool," Officer Lamp said. "Just after we ask you a few questions." He paused for a second before concluding in a loud voice, "Individually."

Justin shrieked.

The officers sent Justin and Mrs. Russo away and sat Max down for their little talk. This was not going to turn out well, Justin thought.

Chapter Six

Harper and the rest of the crowd were staring at Alex. "Did you just say you're a wizard?" Harper asked, walking over to Alex.

Alex thought for a moment. No one outside of her family knew she was a wizard-in-training. Then she said, "I want to say no, but yes, I did say I was a wizard." She couldn't lie. She had done this to herself by casting the truth spell.

"You think you're a wizard?" Harper asked, a little alarmed.

"Yeah," Alex said in a dismissive tone, "but everybody's saying crazy stuff right now. I want Gigi to say some stuff to you now." She was trying hard to redirect Harper's attention.

One of Gigi's friends suddenly broke the silence Alex's revelation had caused by saying, "The truth is, I hate wearing this dress!" She ripped it off to reveal shorts and a tank top, and then she gasped at what she had done.

"You want to know what I want to do? I want to break this," Alex said holding up a plate.

"Do it!" all the girls exclaimed. Alex dropped the plate and it shattered on the floor.

"That felt good," Alex admitted.

"You know what I've always really wanted to do?" Gigi said, walking over to one of the tables. "This!" Then she grabbed one end of the tablecloth and yanked it. The beautifully set tabletop came crashing down and everyone in the room gasped.

"Great idea, Gigi," one of her friends said,

before doing the exact same thing to another table.

Then another girl said, "That looks like fun!" She did the same thing at yet another table. Soon many of the girls were pulling tablecloths from perfectly set tables and making a giant mess of the whole room. Harper was devastated.

"Stop! Stop!" she yelled. "All I wanted was a tea, with sandwiches and gloves and small talk that no one would remember when they got home."

"Well," Alex said, approaching her friend, "that isn't what this tea's about! And I know you won't believe me, but you're going to have to believe Gigi. *Gigi*!" Alex searched the crowd frantically.

But just then the hostess hurried into the room with a serious look on her face. "Ladies! Ladies!" she called over the girls' chatter.

Harper let out a big sigh of relief. "Finally! Someone to restore order."

"No," the hostess said. "Here's something I've always wanted to do!" She grabbed a chair and climbed up on it. Then she took a big leap and grabbed on to the giant chandelier hanging from the middle of the ceiling and started swinging. *Whoo! Whoo!*

She clearly wasn't there to restore order.

Back at the Russos' apartment, the officers had just begun to question Max. "How you doing today, Max?" Officer Lamp asked, taking a seat beside him on the couch.

"I'm fine, thanks," Max replied nervously.

"Is it okay if I call you Maxy?" the officer said. "I got a note here that says they sometimes call you Maxy."

"Yeah, Maxy's cool. I'm trying out Maximillions, though. See if it catches on—"

"That's great, Maxy," Officer Lamp interrupted.

"I—I guess it's not catching on," Max stuttered.

"Are those shoes new?" Lamp continued.

"No. You sure you don't want to try out Maximillions?"

"I'm done with him, goblin," Officer Lamp shouted. "Get him out of here!"

Max ran out of the room, screaming.

Next it was Justin's turn. He sat down beside the goblin who stared at him so long that Justin felt they were in a staring competition with each other.

"So, Justin," Officer Lamp started, standing over him, "word on the street is that you're the best student, regular and wizard school."

"I do okay," Justin said, finally breaking away from the goblin's stare.

"I guess that means you're smart enough to realize that Maxy, cute kid, told us the whole story. And if your story doesn't exactly match his, well, we're going to have a problem." The officer bent down, putting himself face-to-face with Justin.

Justin cringed and waved his hand in front of his nose. The officer's breath wasn't exactly fresh. Justin knew what Officer Lamp and the goblin were up to, and he wasn't falling for it. "I don't know what you're talking about. We didn't do anything," he said.

"Get out of here!" Officer Lamp yelled.

"I'll go when I'm ready," Justin replied calmly.

But the goblin detective had other ideas. He started to shout at Justin in goblin language. Justin quickly changed his mind and ran out of the room.

The last to be questioned was Mrs. Russo. She sat on the couch nervously, while the officers stared at her. "Theresa Russo," Officer Lamp began ominously. "Mortal, married to former wizard Jerry Russo."

"Yeah, you have a couple of nice kids," the goblin said earnestly.

Though there was no pressure on her,

Mrs. Russo caved in a hurry. "We did it!" she shouted. "I mean, they did it! But I let them into the lair, so I guess we did it."

The goblin looked at her. "We? I? Who was it, lady?" he demanded.

"It was me, but they drove me to it," she pleaded. "There was leg-shaking and ear-flicking, and I had to do the bank deposit! Do you have any idea how hard it is to run a business from your home!"

"Tell you what we're going to do," Officer Lamp started.

"You're going to let me off with a warning, because I'm not a wizard, and I didn't know any better," Mrs. Russo suggested, hopefully.

"What, are you living in a fantasy world?" the goblin said.

Mrs. Russo had a puzzled look on her face. She thought that was certainly an odd question for a goblin to ask the mother of three wizards-in-training.

Chapter Seven

While Mrs. Russo, Max, and Justin awaited their sentence at home downtown, Alex still had some unfinished business to take care of at the party.

The hostess was still swinging from the chandelier as all the guests watched. "I feel so free! I hate The Hotel Fleur d'*Blaeglublaflu-flaaeghflaa*!" she shouted gleefully.

Harper was completely beside herself. "Stop it! You have no manners!" she shouted.

Alex stepped in. "I know this isn't going the way you want it to, but this is what had to happen. Gigi, why don't you tell everybody the real reason why you had this stupid tea in the first place?"

Alex's spell was still in full effect, and Gigi was brutally honest as a result. "Okay, that's easy," she said. "See, the truth is, this tea is really a contest to see who can bring the biggest loser. And I brought Harper, and she was just about to be crowned winner."

Harper was stunned. "You think I'm the biggest loser?" she asked quietly. "So the sleep-overs and snickerdoodles, that was a lie?"

"Yeah," Gigi said bluntly. "We were just trying to string you along and get you to come to this loser tea."

Harper turned to Alex then, realizing what her friend had been trying to do. "And you didn't come for the tea. You came to protect me," she said incredulously.

"I'll always protect you," Alex said. "It's what we do."

Gigi looked at one of her wannabe friends then. "You know, it's funny," she said. "You brought Nellie when Nellie really should've brought you," she said. Everyone gasped at how mean Gigi could be. Even worse, because of the spell, Alex knew Gigi was speaking the truth.

"See that?" Alex said to the wannabe. "Gigi thinks you're a bigger loser, and you're supposedly her friend."

Gigi's "friend" wasn't just going to stand there and take that. "Oh, you think I'm a loser?" she said to Gigi, reaching for a big chocolate cake that was sitting on the dessert table. "Well, this is what I think of you." She held the cake up in the air.

Again, everyone gasped at the scene unfolding before them. Alex stepped up to the girl and said, "Now, what do you want to do with that cake?"

"I want to eat it?" the girl asked her timidly.

Alex sighed. "Okay. What's the second thing you want to do with that cake?"

"Throw it at Gigi!" she cried. And she pushed the whole cake right in Gigi's face. Gigi was covered in dark chocolate, her eyes barely visible. She just stood there fuming while the crowd laughed until another girl approached her.

"I don't like Gigi, either," she said.

Alex was happy to help. "Here," she said, handing her a pitcher of iced tea.

The girl took the pitcher with enthusiasm. "I think that it's time that Gigi gets a taste of what she's been dishing out to all of us for years," she said as she hoisted the pitcher above Gigi's head and started to pour.

"No, no!" Gigi gasped as the cold liquid splashed over her.

Shrieks and screams of joy echoed around the room, and Alex suddenly felt that she had to put an end to Gigi's humiliation. "Stop, everybody! Stop! I honestly think I may have gone too far," she called out.

"You think?" Gigi said sarcastically, spitting out chocolate cake and iced tea.

"But I know someone who hasn't," Alex continued. "Harper." She handed her the loser crown.

Harper looked at her friend, puzzled. "You want me to wear the loser crown?" she asked. "Well, okay." She took the crown from Alex and was about to put it on her head.

"No!" Alex yelled and pointed her in the direction of Gigi.

"Oh! Okay." Harper finally understood. She walked over to their once-again nemesis and crowned her the biggest loser of her own biggest-loser party. It was classic.

"Hmm," Harper said to Alex, admiring their work. "Well, it's not exactly the tea I imagined, but I'll never forget it. Let's go home."

"Not yet," Alex said. "There's something I saw that I kind of want to do before we leave."

The next thing Harper knew, she and Alex were both swinging from the chandelier along with the hostess.

"*Whee!*" they yelled as they swung back and forth.

"You guys know you have to clean all this up, right?" the hostess said.

"We kind of figured," Harper replied.

"And pay for everything you broke?" the hostess added.

"That's fair," Alex said. "Can we do two more swings?"

"Sure," she said. And the three of them stayed there a while, swinging happily and laughing about the not-so-elegant tea party.

Downtown at the Russos' house, Mrs. Russo, Justin, and Max were downstairs in the lair paying for their prank by doing community service. Their wards were wearing comfy robes as they watched the Russos wash their clothes in a big laundry cauldron.

"How is washing their laundry community service?" Justin asked.

"We're part of the community, aren't we?" Officer Lamp responded.

"Oh, that's bunk," Max said.

Mrs. Russo pulled out a shirt with more than two sleeves.

"Hey, careful with that. That's my wife's," the goblin said.

"Oh, it . . . it's lovely," Mrs. Russo said, smiling. "She must be very, uh, handy."

She turned to her two sons and made a face. She knew what she'd gotten herself into by marrying a former wizard. But she certainly hoped that her wizards-in-training laid off the magical pranks for a while.

PART
TWO

Chapter One

Justin was heading to his locker after his last class of the day, when his classmate Brian stopped him. "Justin, way to score on the world history exam," he said.

"Oh, thanks, Brian," Justin said, grateful for the compliment. But he was a little confused, too. After all, Brian was Mr. Popularity. "You know, uh, this might sound kinda lame, but I didn't think you knew my name."

"I didn't," Brian said. "You left your sweater in class. It has your name in it. Look, I didn't do so good on this test," Brian admitted as Justin opened his locker. "I just got one right." He paused, embarrassed. "My name."

"Look," Brian continued. "I was wondering if you could help me out. You know, tutor me."

"I don't know. I'm kind of busy," Justin told him.

"I'll give you two tickets to the Tears of Blood concert," Brian offered. Tears of Blood was the hottest new rock band, and tickets to their concerts were hard to come by.

"T.O.B? Their new tour is awesome!" Justin was thrilled. He slammed the door to his locker. "You got a deal. Come by the Sub Station after school." T.O.B. was Justin's favorite band. He couldn't believe his good luck—a little tutoring would be a snap, especially if it meant free T.O.B. tickets!

"Awesome," Brian said, relieved. Then he

said in a very threatening, tough-guy kind of way, "Oh, uh, if any of my friends ask you, I was all over you for talking to my girlfriend."

Justin considered this for a minute before assuming the same tough-guy tone with Brian. "And if any of my friends ask you, your girl-friend actually talked to me."

Harper and Alex were on the way to their lockers when Harper got a message on her phone. "Oh, my gosh, did you hear?" Harper gushed. "The 'Gurt Barn's giving out free frozen yogurt samples."

"Oh. How do you know that?" Alex asked, wondering where that info had suddenly come from.

"On my cell," Harper told her. "I got a 'Gurt Alert." She giggled.

"Well, you're going to have to try it without me," Alex said with a shrug. "I have to work."

Harper scoffed. "You always have to work,"

she whined. Harper was annoyed because she had to do fun things like going to the 'Gurt Barn on her own. It would have been so much more fun to share free samples with her best friend.

Before Alex could respond, a guy walked by them wearing a beanie. The two girls looked at each other.

"A beanie?" Alex asked, with an amused smile. Then, right there in the middle of the hallway, the two girls broke into a song and dance routine they had done for years:

"What's that? A hat?
Crazy, funky, junky hat?
Overslept? Hair unsightly?
Trying to look like Keira Knightley?
We've been there, we've done that.
We see right through your funky hat!"

When they finished the routine, they started talking normally again as if they hadn't just been jumping around, high-fiving, and bumping hips to their silly hat song.

"You were saying?" Alex asked.

"It's just really hard to have a friend who's always busy," Harper grumbled. She didn't want to make Alex feel bad about having to work, but Harper really did wish they could spend a little more time together.

"I know," Alex agreed. But then she got an idea. "Ooh, why don't I get my parents to give you a job at the sandwich shop? That way we can hang out all the time and even get paid for it." Alex couldn't believe she hadn't thought of this sooner. This was one of the best ideas she'd ever had.

"Really? That'd be great. I've never had a job before. Well, except for the dollar Grandma gives me for rubbing lotion on her feet."

"Yeah, well, we'll just make sure that you're wearing gloves when you make the sandwiches," Alex joked.

Chapter Two

The two girls had a lot of scheming to do if this was going to work. Alex and Harper knew that Alex's parents weren't exactly looking for more help, so they had devised a plan to convince Mr. and Mrs. Russo to hire Harper anyway. They had to make the Russos think that Harper would be invaluable to the restaurant.

Alex was hanging out with her parents

inside the Sub Station that afternoon when Harper walked in. She was wearing a T-shirt with an appliquéd sandwich on it and carrying a HELP WANTED sign. It had been Alex's idea, and she thought it was pretty clever.

"Good afternoon, Mr. and Mrs. Russo," Harper said cheerfully. She headed right up to the counter where Mrs. Russo was drying some baskets. "I happened to be passing by when I noticed this HELP WANTED sign. I'd like to apply for the position."

"Oh, wow," Alex chimed in as she approached the counter. "I didn't know we were hiring. What a good idea, Mom and Dad."

"Harper, we didn't put that sign in the window," Mr. Russo told her as he headed off to clear a table.

"Well, someone must have," Alex said innocently.

"We're not hiring any sandwich associates," Mr. Russo said.

"Or people wearing a sandwich," Mrs. Russo added, noting Harper's T-shirt.

Mr. Russo suddenly became very serious when he said, "Harper, there's no job available. But if you can turn that sandwich into a taco, I think Raul's is hiring down the street."

Alex wasn't ready to let this go so fast, though. "But we're swamped," she protested. "We totally need more help with . . ." She looked around at the empty restaurant. This was going to be a hard case to make at this hour of the day. Suddenly an idea dawned. "All of our phone orders," she finished, satisfied with her own quick thinking.

Mrs. Russo looked at Alex and Harper sympathetically. "Girls, I know you think it'd be fun to work together, but it's really hard to work with friends . . . or family. The one time you forget to wipe off the tip of the mustard squeeze bottle, it's suddenly three hours of silent salami slicing," she said, recounting an incident between her and Mr. Russo from their early days of running the restaurant.

"It—it dries at the end and gets crusty. It's unsightly," Mr. Russo argued. The Russos stared at each other as if they were reliving their fight all over again.

Alex tried to shake off her parents' strange walk down memory lane. "But Mom, Dad, think about it. If Harper works here, you guys could spend more time with each other," Alex said, working a new angle entirely. She was nothing if not fast on her feet.

"Yeah, Jerry," Mrs. Russo said, starting to get on board. "We could even go to one of those, uh, dollar movies you're always talking about."

"It's a movie for a dollar," Mr. Russo said, getting excited about the idea. "How could you *not* talk about that?"

"Let me show you," Mrs. Russo said to her husband. Then she abruptly turned back to her daughter. "Alex, it is a big responsibility training a new employee."

"Does that mean yes?" Alex said, her voice rising with excitement.

"You can't shirk your responsibilities while you're training her," Mr. Russo said, finally coming around to the idea as well.

"Does that mean yes?" Alex asked again, leaning over the counter, practically jumping out of her skin.

"And remember, business comes before friendship," Mrs. Russo said.

"I'm taking this all as a yes," Alex said, turning to Harper. "Harper, you're hired." The two girls let out a huge shriek and started laughing and jumping up and down.

But they quickly straightened themselves out, remembering what Alex's parents had said. "I mean, welcome to our family's business," Alex said, giving Harper a hearty handshake.

* * *

The next day was Harper's first day of work, and the two girls weren't exactly getting much actual work done. They were sitting at one of the tables, flipping through magazines, as if there weren't a customer in the restaurant that needed attending to. "This would look great on you," Harper said to Alex, pointing to an outfit in her magazine.

Alex glanced at it and said, "No, it'd look better on you. You're more of a summer."

"Speaking of Summer, did you hear what happened to her in gym today?" Harper asked.

"Speaking of Jim, I heard he and Summer are going out now," Alex replied.

"That's what I was gonna say," Harper said.

Mr. Russo was watching the whole exchange and getting more annoyed by the second. "Uh, Regis, Kelly," he said, crouching down to their level, "can I interrupt the talk show to interest you in some actual work?"

"Oh, yeah," Alex said, realizing their mistake. "Sorry, Dad. We were just taking a little break. But we're getting back to work right now."

"Okay," Mr. Russo said letting them off the hook this time. "Well, there's a customer. Why don't you go take his order?"

When Alex saw what the customer was wearing, she turned to Harper.

"A cowboy hat," Alex said, as Harper got into position next to her. Then they launched into the hat song and dance routine.

"What's that? A hat?
Crazy, funky, junky hat?
Overslept? Hair unsightly?
Trying to look like Keira Knightley?
We've been there, we've done that.
We see right through your funky hat!"

Mr. Russo looked on in disbelief. "Wow. I

was one away from having all boys," he lamented.

Alex quickly gathered herself and headed over to the customer's table, Harper in tow. "Hi," she said. "Welcome to Waverly Sub Station. I'm Alex, I'll be your server today. And this is Harper; she's our new trainee."

"Well, I'm thrilled," the guy said mocking Alex's cheerful tone. Clearly he couldn't have cared less who his server, or her new trainee, was. "Tell you what, just gimme the Bronx-strami, a large root beer, and a slice of that coffee cake over there, huh?"

Harper quickly piped up, "Really? Here's what I do: I get the half order, because it's just as filling and half the price—"

Alex was horrified. Harper was trying to get the customer to order less! Alex knew her parents would freak out if they overheard her. "Harper!"

"What?" Harper said, still oblivious. "That's

what I do. Oh, and get the small soda, because it's free refills," she added.

"Harper," Alex said even louder, "when I said, 'Harper,' I meant stop talking." Harper just shrugged.

"Yeah, I'll have what the trainee said, huh?" the guy said, having taken Harper's advice into consideration.

When the girls got back to the lunch counter, Harper looked at Alex hopefully. "How'd I do?" she asked.

"Well," Alex replied, "you just turned a twelve-dollar order into us owing him!" She was so frustrated! But there was no time to explain now. The restaurant was getting very busy, and the girls had to spring into action.

"Table four, sandwich up!" Mr. Russo yelled out as he rang the pickup bell. Alex figured she'd better keep a close eye on Harper. "Look," she said, "why don't you just run sandwiches while I take the orders." Alex figured there would be less for Harper to screw up this way. After all, how hard could it be to deliver sandwiches to the tables?

But as soon as Harper got her hands on a sandwich basket, it went flying across the room and splattered onto the floor. "Oh! I'm sorry," she said.

"Look, why don't you just clean tables, and I'll take orders and run the sandwiches?" Alex suggested.

Mrs. Russo came over to Alex then. "So, how's Harper working out?" she asked.

"Great," Alex lied. "She's really getting the hang of it."

But then, just when Alex's mom was looking, Harper had to go and prove her wrong. Harper was behind the counter with the cowboy-hat guy's coffee cake on a plate in front of her when she said, "How much coffee do I pour on the coffee cake?" Alex saw that Harper was holding the coffeepot over the cake and laughed to throw her mom off. "That's just a joke between me and her." Then she looked at Harper directly and said in a loud whisper, "None, Harper, none!"

The rest of the afternoon was positively painful, especially for Mr. Russo. Harper's first attempt at waitressing consisted mostly of people getting the wrong food, or else people getting food dumped on them—especially Mr. Russo. He had changed his shirt several times already when one last domino effect caused by his wreckless new employee sent him over the edge. By the end of the day, Mr. Russo's fourth shirt was dripping with chili and ketchup, and he had had quite enough of his daughter's little experiment. He gritted his teeth and said, "Alex, can I talk to you in the kitchen?"

"Um, are you sure you don't want to change your shirt first? It's kind of gross," Alex suggested.

Mr. Russo did not think this was funny at all. He had lost his sense of humor two shirts ago. "No," he said, angrily. "Because I'm sure she's going to do it again."

Mrs. Russo came into the kitchen with them, and now both of Alex's parents were standing before her, arms crossed, about to give her a really hard time about Harper. "Look," Alex started, "before you guys talk about whatever you want to talk about, I have something to say. Harper's not working out."

"Oh, good," Mr. Russo said. "Then we're on the same page."

"I'm not sure where this is going, but continue," Mrs. Russo said.

"Right. I think we should let Harper go," Alex said. She couldn't take it anymore—Harper was causing her to do more work, not less.

Mrs. Russo let out a sigh of relief, and Mr. Russo said, "Okay, this is a lot easier than I thought it was going to be."

"Yeah. Let me know how she takes it," Alex

said, about to dash back into the dining room. She was trying to get out of having to fire Harper herself. Mrs. Russo was on to her, though.

"Okay," Mrs. Russo said loudly, stopping Alex in her tracks. "Now we're not on the same page. It was your idea to hire Harper. And we told you, business before friendship. So you're going to have to fire her."

"Well, now, I have a problem with that," Alex said. "You two come with me," she commanded, opening the door to the storage room and ushering her parents inside. "Go," she urged.

"What are we doing in here?" Mrs. Russo asked, once they were all inside with the door closed.

"Okay. If we stay in here long enough, Harper won't be able to find anyone, and she'll just leave," Alex explained.

"And you expect that to work?" Mr. Russo asked.

"Well, it's how I got out of Harper's sewing club," Alex told them.

Mrs. Russo opened the door. "Look, if Harper's not better by the end of the day, you're going to have to fire her," she told her daughter firmly.

"And I don't know how you're going to do it," Mr. Russo added, "but I agree with your mother."

"Fine," Alex said. "But this could've worked." Her parents went back to the dining room, but Alex ran downstairs to the wizard lair to get a spell book. There had to be one that could get her out of this!

Chapter Three

Alex came up a few minutes later flipping through a giant, dusty spell book. "Waitress spell . . . waitress spell . . . no waitress spell," she groaned. Then she stopped on something. "Serving *wrench*?" she said skeptically. She blew some of the dust away. "Oh, serving wench," she realized. Right then Justin walked in. "Hey," Alex said to her book-smart older brother, "what's a serving wench?"

"Serving wench," Justin said, as if he were a

talking dictionary. "A young woman, usually related to an innkeeper, who, during medieval times, would serve grog and food to guests of the inn."

"So, like a waitress, right?" Alex asked.

"Well, not technically. Because—" Justin started to explain. He was always very thorough. But before he had the chance, his little sister cut him off.

"But, like a waitress, right?" she asked, hopefully.

"I guess. Why? Did Dad say there's a pop quiz on the medieval food-service industry?" He was starting to get paranoid, like the overachieving student he was.

"Yep, better study up," Alex recommended, knowing full well she was playing a not-so-nice joke on her brother. Knowing him, he'd probably cram everything he could about the medieval food-service industry into his head by the time he went to bed that night.

Meanwhile, Alex headed back into the dining room and observed her serving-skills-challenged friend making one last mistake. "Um, I had a diet," her customer was saying.

"Are you sure that's not a diet?" Harper asked. Then she picked up the woman's soda and took a sip. Next she picked up the soda of the guy sitting next to the woman and took a sip of his. Then she switched the glasses! "You're right," she said with a sigh. "That's not the diet. This is the diet. There. All better?" The customers were horrified.

Alex couldn't believe her eyes. If she didn't fix this quickly, she would have to fire her best friend, and there was no way she could handle that. Alex decided she better try out the serving-wench spell. She took a deep breath and said, *Take this girl with the skills of a bench and turn her into a serving wench.*

Now Harper took a fresh look at those same customers and said to them, "You know, you need all-new drinks. I'll get those right away."

"So, how are you doing?" Alex asked Harper as she approached the counter.

"Suddenly, a lot better," Harper replied cheerfully.

Suddenly was right. In one split second, Harper went from being a super screw-up to being a superwaitress. She was carrying six or seven platters above her head, throwing one of them up in the air while she grabbed a soda and catching it at just the right time. It was amazing to watch, which is what Alex and her parents did for the rest of the day. Harper barely needed any help at all now, so they stood there, mouths hanging open in disbelief at the sudden transformation.

"Boy, Harper improved quickly," Mr. Russo said to Alex, having witnessed that last move.

"Yeah, well, sometimes it just takes a while for your skills to kick in. You probably know that from coaching, since you're such a good coach," Alex said. She hoped her father would be swayed by her flattery and wouldn't start to question how Harper had gotten to be such a good waitress so fast.

"I am a pretty good coach," Mr. Russo said, patting himself on the back.

Alex smiled to herself.

Meanwhile, across the alley, in the extra seating area of the Sub Station, Justin had taken over some tables and renamed them the "Brain Train." He had really gotten into the idea of tutoring, and by that afternoon he had rounded up a lot of clients. He was walking around the room, checking on their work.

"Okay, uh, Greg. It's great that you 'heart' Cindy, but that's not going to help you in algebra class," he chided, before moving on to Anthony, who he was helping with a writing assignment. "Anthony, you're going to have to start all over. Just saying that the Empire State Building is tall and pointy is not an essay. It's barely a sentence."

Then he made his way over to Natalie. He was helping her build a model of a water molecule out of lollipops. "And Natalie," he said, "this is H_3O." He took a lollipop off her model and popped it in his mouth. "Now it's H_2O, and I have a treat," he said, smiling.

Just then, Frankie, the neighborhood bully, walked in. Well, it wasn't that he really was the neighborhood bully—he was maybe ten years old and about four feet tall—so much as he *thought* he was the neighborhood bully. "Oh, what can I help you with, young man?" Justin asked.

"First of all, it's what I can help *you* with," Frankie said, in his usual "gangster" tone of voice. "This is a great tutoring business you got here. It'd be a shame to see something happen to it." He looked at Justin pointedly, hoping Justin understood his veiled threat. Then, he took a swipe at Justin's globe, which went tumbling to the floor as a result.

"What?" Justin screeched, shocked at the younger kid's behavior.

"Oops," Frankie shrugged. "Looks like your world's come tumbling down."

"You owe me a new globe," Justin demanded.

"No, you owe me twenty-five percent of your tutoring action," Frankie countered. "I'm the tutor in this neighborhood, and I don't like competition."

"I bet you also don't like amusement parks, 'cause you're not tall enough to ride the rides," Justin chided him, holding his hand flat over Frankie's head as if he were the height-measuring bar at one of the rides.

"Witty comeback," Frankie admitted. "You know what I think of witty comebacks?" He knocked over a giant can of pencils.

"Oh, what a—" Justin started to yell

something, but Frankie interrupted him.

"Pick up those sticks. Get it? It's a game. Look it up." Then he motioned for Justin to come down to his level. When Justin obliged, Frankie patted him on the cheek. "Good day," Frankie said, before walking out of the room.

"You get 'em. You're closer to the ground," Justin started to yell after him, but he was already gone. "'Cause he's . . ." He started to explain his joke to the other kids but gave up quickly. He wasn't sure how he would handle Frankie, but he knew he'd think of something. Right now, he had to study for the pop quiz on medieval food service that Alex had clued him in on.

Chapter Four

That evening at the restaurant, Alex's spell was still in full effect.

"Two on a raft Brooklyn style; burn 'em!" Harper yelled back to the kitchen. "I need a roast beef; knock the wind out of it and let it walk!" It was like she had been waitressing for her entire life, plus another. Since medieval times, Alex thought.

Mr. and Mrs. Russo walked into the restaurant

then and looked around with great surprise. The place was packed.

"Where did all these people come from?" Mrs. Russo asked with a big smile on her face.

"Oh," Alex said from behind the counter. "Harper gave everyone who was here earlier a coupon to come back for dinner and get a free soda with every sandwich."

"But we already give free soda at dinner," Mr. Russo said, confused.

"I know," Alex said. "She's brilliant."

They all watched then as Harper rocked the dinner hour, managing all the orders, sending plates flying through the air from behind the counter to just the right customers, managing to take care of the entire place without a hitch. She barely even needed Alex around to help waitress!

For the rest of the night, the Russos barely had to do anything—it was like Harper was managing *them*.

"Harper is doing great," Mrs. Russo said as they started to clean up.

"I know," Alex said, forming a plan in her head. "You know what you should do? You should leave her in charge tomorrow so that you and Dad could spend the day doing something."

"You know, for as long as we've lived in New York, we've never been to the Statue of Liberty," Mr. Russo said. They had spent so much time taking care of the kids and getting the restaurant in order that it rarely occurred to them to take a day off.

"I know," Mrs. Russo agreed. "And it's the one pencil sharpener missing from my monument collection."

"Let's go!" Mr. Russo cheered.

"Order's up!" Harper yelled from behind the counter.

Alex ran over to her. "Oh, my gosh. Did you hear that? I just talked my mom and dad into leaving you in charge. So when they leave, we can lock up, and we can do whatever we want." She paused for a moment, before adding, "Except go to the Statue of Liberty."

"I don't think so," Harper said. "We're going to be pretty busy here. I just e-mailed out a breakfast special, so you should be in about five a.m."

Alex was taken aback and quickly scoffed at Harper's suggestion. "I'm not coming in at five a.m." Harper was missing the point. They were supposed to slack off and have a fun day together.

"Yeah. I think you are," Harper said in a very bossy tone. Then she yelled back to the kitchen. "I need two bow-wows painted red, and who do I have to kick in the can to get some nachos?"

Alex was getting mad now. "I can come in whenever I want," she said to Harper.

"No, you can't," Harper said. "You heard

your parents. They're leaving me in charge."

"Because I told them to," Alex explained. "You're not my boss. I checked with my boss, and since I am the boss of me, I'm giving myself the day off," she said and stomped away. She couldn't believe her best friend was acting this way now. This was no fun at all.

Harper stepped out from behind the counter. "I hate to do this," she said, approaching Alex, "but if you don't come in tomorrow, you're fired."

"You can't fire me. It's my family's restaurant. You're fired," Alex shot back.

Now it was Harper's turn to laugh. "I'm in charge. You can't fire me."

"My family owns the restaurant," Alex said, getting a little bossy herself, "and since I'm in the family, that makes me part owner. Owners can fire employees. Do the math."

"Well, fine. If you fire me from the

restaurant, I'm firing you . . . from being my friend," Harper yelled before walking out the door.

Alex could only let out a big sigh before heading back to the counter to tell her parents what had happened. She saw how busy they were and decided to wait until the dinner rush had calmed down before she told them. Once they were all cleaned up and things had settled down, she told them the whole story. Now she was sitting at the counter with her head in her hands as they all talked about it.

"So, did she quit, or did you fire her? Which is it?" Mr. Russo was extremely interested in the specifics.

"It was complicated. I guess both," Alex told him. She wasn't really sure how it happened. All she knew was that she was very disappointed that things had turned out this way. She had just wanted them to have a good time working together. And to think, she had saved Harper's job by putting that spell on her!

"Well, make sure she quit," he pleaded. "That way I don't have to pay her for the rest of the week."

"Jerry!" Mrs. Russo scolded her husband for his insensitivity.

"Oh," he said, realizing his mistake. "I mean, I'm sorry. It's hard to work with friends." It was a halfhearted attempt, which Alex and Mrs. Russo had seen through, so he headed back into the kitchen, leaving Alex and her mom by themselves.

"So," Mrs. Russo said, putting her elbow on the counter. "You think you and Harper are going to be okay?"

"I don't know. I tried to fire her from the job, but she fired me from being her friend," Alex said with a big sigh.

They both noticed a girl in a cute red hat then, and Alex tried to sing the hat song by herself. "*What's that? A hat? Crazy, funky, junky . . .*" Her voice trailed off. It was no use. "Ah, forget it. It's not the same."

"Oh, honey," her mom said kindly, "you want me to do that crazy hat dance with you?" Then she proceeded do some of the dorkiest dance moves anyone could possibly do.

Alex was certain she didn't want to do the hat dance with her mother. "No," she said. "It'd be weird. It's kinda me and Harper's thing. And sometimes it's about you," she said with a little smirk.

Chapter Five

The next night, Justin had his new Brain Train crew outside the restaurant in the alley. "And for our next experiment," he said to them, "Chris is going to drop a water balloon and a Ping-Pong ball from upstairs at the same time. Which one do you think is going to hit the ground first?"

But before anyone could answer, a water balloon came crashing down on Justin's head. "Chris!" he yelled in the direction of the roof.

"You were supposed to wait for me to say 'go'!" He looked at the group then. "That guy—" he started to say before getting hit again with another water balloon. "Okay. Kinda deserved that one. Let's take five and regroup." The minute the jocks were out of sight, Frankie appeared.

"Looks like Galileo's all wet," he said to Justin. "Where's my cut? The Answer Man's getting tired of waiting." Besides being the neighborhood bully, Frankie was also known as the Answer Man.

"You're tired?" Justin asked, feigning concern. "Sounds like it's nap time for the Answer Man," he joked.

"Nap time," Frankie nodded. "Good one. Maybe it's nap time for you!" he said, his voice rising. "Enforcers, assemble!" he yelled, and a bunch of little kids came out of nowhere. One of them descended from a rooftop on a rope and then got into his fighting position.

"So, you've got a lot of really tiny friends." Justin laughed. "And anyone can drop down a rope and . . ."

Frankie interrupted him and pointed to the kids standing next to him. "These two guys have black belts in tae kwon do," he said ominously. "That guy brought a rope."

Justin wasn't taking this. "Chris," he yelled to the rooftop, "let 'em all go!"

On cue, tons of water balloons and Ping-Pong balls came crashing down on Frankie and his boys.

"Retreat, retreat!" Frankie yelled as they all ran off.

Justin laughed as they ran away. It looked like he was the Answer Man now.

Later, Justin was inside the restaurant, looking out the front window for signs of Frankie and his gang, when Alex came down the stairs from the apartment.

She walked over to him quietly and poked him on the shoulder. "Justin," she whispered.

But Justin, in fighting mode, hopped into a ninja pose and let out a battle cry before realizing it was his sister. "Oh, it's you," he said casually. "Hey, you haven't seen like four or five tiny little ninjas running around, have ya?"

"No. Have you seen really tall flowers that talk?" Alex asked, acting like she had gone down the rabbit hole and was now in Wonderland. "Wait," she said, noting Justin's confused expression. "I'm not sure what game we're playing."

"Look, there's this kid, Frankie," he started to explain to Alex. "He and his little thugs are after me. They're trying to muscle in on my Brain Train action."

Alex just shrugged. She had no idea what Justin was talking about. She had been so involved with the restaurant and Harper that she didn't even know what the Brain Train was. "Oh, this isn't as fun a game as I thought."

"Hey, ah, are you on your way to see Harper?" Justin asked her.

"No. Why? Where have you seen Harper?" Alex asked, suddenly very interested in what her brother had to say.

"Well, when Frankie chased me earlier, I hid in the 'Gurt Barn. She works there now. She wouldn't let me hide in the bathroom unless I bought something," he explained.

"Huh. So she got a job at 'Gurt Barn," Alex said.

"Yeah, and she's amazing," Justin said. "She had, like, ten waffle cones and a couple of 'Gurt shakes in one hand."

"I did that," Alex admitted to Justin. "I put a spell on her to make her good."

Then it dawned on him. "Wait a minute!" Justin exclaimed. "You used the serving-wench spell on her." He paused then, having another epiphany. "Wait another minute! There's no pop quiz on the medieval food-service industry. I crammed for that!"

"Are you done?" Alex asked impatiently. "'Cause I've got to go apologize to Harper."

"Ye—" Justin started and then stopped to make sure. "Yes," he finally said. "I'm done. Yeah."

Alex headed out to the 'Gurt Barn then, and Justin followed her outside, feeling emboldened enough to confront his tiny nemesis. He had a plan now.

Once everything was in place, Justin just hung out in the alley waiting for Frankie to appear, which he finally did. He and Justin spotted each other right away. "Justin Russo," Frankie said, slowly walking toward him. "You, you thought you could hide, but you can't. Enforcers, assemble!" he yelled into the night air. All the little kids came out of the woodwork. Then Frankie said, "Any last words, Russo? Besides 'Mommy?'"

"Yeah, I got something to say," Justin said. "Underachievers, assemble!"

Then the Brain Train jocks came out from behind him. Only, they weren't exactly quick on the uptake, so they wandered around for a minute trying to figure out what they were supposed to be doing.

"Guys! Over here." Justin directed them with an exasperated laugh. They fell into line behind him, all dressed in their varsity jackets. Justin cleared his throat. "I'd like you to meet my friends. This is Brian. He's currently failing geometry, but being recruited by Canadian football. This is Doug, going into his third year of eleventh grade. All-state wrestler. And this guy? He's got a record. You're smart enough to see where this is going, right, Answer Man?" he asked, gloating.

Frankie approached Justin and they stood face-to-face. Well, not exactly face-to-face—Frankie was much smaller than Justin, after all. "Ah, this is just a little back-and-forth," Frankie said. "You know? Somethin' tutors do. Whaddaya say? Friends?" he offered.

Justin could only chuckle. "I don't think so," he said.

Frankie realized he couldn't talk his way out of this one. "Enforcers, run!" he commanded his little troops. And they all took off running.

"Get 'em!" Justin directed the jocks. "They're getting away! Go!"

Chapter Six

Over at the 'Gurt Barn, Harper was getting all kinds of compliments about her impressive waitressing skills. Her manager, a strange woman to be sure, only had glowing things to say. Although she spoke in the dreariest, most monotonous tone, Harper appreciated her. Especially now that she was Harper's only friend.

The manager stopped Harper on her way

back from delivering an order to a table. "I know you've only been working here four hours," she said, "but congratulations. You're employee of the month. As soon as I get some photo paper . . ." she said and then paused, "go home . . ." she paused again, "hook it up to my printer . . . print it . . . bring it back here . . . I'll pin it up."

"Gee, thanks!" Harper said. The manager may not have been high-energy, but at least she appreciated Harper's amazing waitressing skills.

"It's a real honor," the manager continued. "I almost won it four times. But I didn't . . . 'cause I take too many breaks." She paused again for what seemed like ten minutes. "That reminds me, it's time for my break." Then she walked out, and Harper headed back behind the counter.

Alex walked in while Harper's back was to the door, so when Harper turned around to wait on her, she was taken aback. "Hi, welcome to the 'Gurt Barn. How can I—" She scoffed as soon as she saw who the customer was. "What do you want?" she said, her voice all business and devoid of that 'Gurt Barn charm.

"For us to be friends again," Alex pleaded. "And I'm not leaving here until we are."

"Well, I don't need your friendship, 'cause I'm employee of the month. And I have a new friend," Harper bragged.

"Who?" Alex asked, a little concerned.

"My manager," Harper said.

Alex looked at her friend suspiciously. "Oh, yeah?" she asked. "What's her name?"

"Well, I can't tell you," Harper hedged. "She told me not to wear it out."

"Look, Harper, we're best friends, and just because you got really bossy at the restaurant doesn't mean I don't miss you being my best friend," Alex said. She really wanted this whole fight to go away, but Harper wasn't giving up very easily.

"I wasn't bossy. You weren't respecting me as your boss," Harper said.

This got Alex all riled up again. "Because you're not my boss!" she half-shouted. "Why don't you just accept my apology?" she demanded.

Harper was really annoyed. "Because 'you got really bossy' is not an apology. Now just go away, I have to refill the machine." Harper was still in an all-work-no-play mode, since the spell was still in full effect.

Alex was about to leave when Frankie came running in. "Can I hide in your bathroom?" he asked, out of breath.

"Not unless you buy something," Harper told him.

"I'll pay on the way out," Frankie said, before running off to the bathroom anyway. The minute he was gone, Justin and Brian came in.

"I thought he ran in here," Brian said.

"Where is he?" Justin asked.

"I don't know, but I've got to go to the bathroom," Brian said.

Justin spotted Alex then. "Hey, Alex, how did things go with you and Harper?" he asked her while he waited for Brian, his new body-guard, to come back.

"Not good," Alex said.

"What are you going to do?" Justin asked her.

"I'm doing it," Alex said, and prepared to reverse the spell. *"Take this girl who's a great serving wench and give her back the skills of a bench."*

Harper happened to be carrying dishes of yogurt to a table while Alex chanted the spell. Suddenly, she dropped the bowls all over the place.

"Oh, I'm so sorry. I don't usually do this sort of thing. I'm employee of the month," she told them as she tried to scoop the yogurt off the table and back into the bowls. "Well, this is still good. We can scoop some of it up." Once she saw the looks on their faces, though, she thought better of that plan. "Um, let me just get you some all-new yogurt."

Justin and Alex had retreated to a booth at the side of the restaurant to watch what happened, and they were cringing now, seeing what a mess Harper was making. "So, that was your solution?" Justin asked. "Make her look bad in front of everybody?"

"I don't know. I—I'm mad," Alex tried to explain. "I just want her to be my friend."

"Well, if you want her to be your friend, you got to be a friend to her," Justin told his younger sister.

Alex sighed and stood up. "I hate it when you're right," she said to Justin.

"But you kinda want to thank me," Justin said with a smile.

Alex turned to look back at him. "No," she said flatly.

Behind the counter, Harper was having all kinds of trouble with the yogurt machine. There were four spouts—shaped like a cow's udder—spewing all different colors of yogurt, and they were all running at once. There was yogurt everywhere. "Here," Alex said as she joined Harper behind the counter, "let me help you."

"Why do you want to help me?" Harper asked as the yogurt came streaming out all around them.

"Because I'm your friend," Alex said sweetly. "And you can fire me from being your friend, but you can't fire me from acting like your friend." They smiled at each other then, and Alex started trying to work the machine, or at least attempted to catch some of the sticky stuff. "Here," she said, kneeling down to get under the machine. "Go get cups. We need cups." But the cups weren't enough. The yogurt was coming in a fast, endless stream, and it was running all over the floor. The girls could barely stand up in the sticky, slippery mess. "More cups," Alex said.

"I just can't get this cow to turn off," Harper complained. Nothing she did was helping.

"Eww. Okay. No," Alex said, when she realized the cups weren't working. "We're going to need something bigger!" she said.

"Okay," Harper said and handed her one of her shoes. Though Alex looked at her like she was crazy, she stuck the shoe under the spout. Still, it couldn't collect the yogurt fast enough!

"Okay, bigger. We're going to need something bigger!" she yelled. Then it dawned on her that she was in possession of that something. She knelt all the way down and opened her mouth, trying to catch as much of the yogurt as she could. "Brain freeze!" she yelled as the stuff poured all over her. Then, all of a sudden, it just stopped.

"Oh. It must have run out," Harper said.

"Yeah," Alex said just before a giant blob of red yogurt came pouring down on her head. "Nope," she said, as the machine burped its last dish. "Now it did." Alex stood up, covered in yogurt from head to toe.

"I'm so sorry," Harper said, looking at the mess that used to be Alex.

"Why are you sorry?" Alex asked. "It's like a funky hat," she said with a smile. With that, the girls broke out in song.

"What's that? A hat?
Crazy, funky, junky hat?
Overslept? Hair unsightly?
Trying to look like Keira Knightley?
We've been there, we've done that.
We see right through your funky hat!"

This time, the song was sung through laughter at what a mess they had created, on all accounts.

The manager walked in then and found them and the shop in pretty bad shape.

"I'm sorry," Alex said. "We had a bit of an accident."

"We should get our stories straight before the owner comes in," the manager suggested.

All of a sudden, Frankie came running out of the bathroom shouting, "No, no!" He was being followed by Brian. When they reached the front door, Justin hopped out of his seat.

"Hey, wait up!" he yelled and darted out the door behind them.

"We'll blame him," the manager said flatly.

"Perfect," Alex agreed. "I've been blaming him my whole life."

They all laughed, and Alex was so happy that things finally felt like they were getting back to normal. Normal that is, except for the fact that frozen yogurt was dripping from every part of her.

The next day, Alex and Harper did something Mrs. Russo had been asking them to do for a very long time . . . they tried to teach her the hat dance. But Alex's mom just didn't get it. No matter how hard they tried, it just wasn't working out.

They were in the living room of the Russos' loft above the restaurant; Mrs. Russo was standing in front of the girls as they sang the end of the song for what felt like the zillionth time. "*We see right through your funky hat*," they sang, trying not to laugh at Mrs. Russo, who was busy embellishing the girls' moves.

"Mom, don't add your own moves," Alex pleaded. "This isn't the eighties. This isn't *Footgrease* music."

"It's *Footloose* or *Grease*," Mrs. Russo explained seriously. "And those movies were great! Come on. Take it from the top," she said cheerfully.

Without any enthusiasm whatsoever, the girls sang:

"What's that? A hat?
Crazy, funky, junky hat?
Overslept? Hair unsightly?"

But as they sang, Alex and Harper tiptoed out of the room and away from Mrs. Russo, who, by this time, had gotten into mimicking a classic scene from the eighties movie *Flashdance*. *"Trying to look like Keira Knightley?"* she sang. "And, pull the cord! Pull the cord! Pull the cord!" She chanted, leaning all the way back on a chair and pulling an imaginary cord, which in the movie released a rush of water. You can take the girl out of the eighties, but you can't take the eighties out of the girl!

Something magical is on the way!
Look for the next book in Disney's
Wizards of Waverly Place series.

Top of the Class

Adapted by Heather Alexander

Based on the series created by Todd J. Greenwald

Part One is based on the episode, "Wizard School Part I," Written by Vince Cheung & Ben Montanio

Part Two is based on the episode, "Wizard School Part II," Written by Gigi McCreery & Perry Rein

Alex Russo had a huge smile across her face. Today was the best day of the year. It was even better than Christmas. Even better than her birthday. Maybe even better, she thought, than Christmas and her birthday *combined*.

It was the last day of school!

Just thinking about the day made her smile. No homework, no tests, and no teachers for two whole glorious months! Alex pushed her long dark hair out of her eyes and darted through the crowded hallway of Tribeca Prep. Kids whooped and celebrated as they cleaned out their lockers. She waved to her best friend, Harper Evans, and then hurried over to her sixteen-year-old brother, Justin.

As Justin pulled a book from his locker, Alex peeked in and gasped. His locker was so neat, so organized, so . . . unlike her locker. She hadn't dared open her own locker in two days. There was a pretty good chance that a year's worth of forgotten homework assignments and worksheets would tumble out and bury her.

"How was your last day of school, Alex?" Justin asked.

Alex sighed. "Oh, tough. So many people were signing my yearbook, I ran out of room. I had to get a second yearbook." She glanced at the blue leather book in her hands.

"How did you get a second yearbook?"

Justin asked suspiciously. "They're all gone." As soon as he said it, Justin knew the answer. He searched his locker. Just as he had suspected— his yearbook was missing. "Where's my year-book, Alex?"

"Come on, Justin," Alex replied. "Hardly anybody signed it, and one of them was you."

"Yeah . . ." Justin stalled for time. It wasn't easy having a sister who was one of the most popular girls in school. "Maybe I was saving room for friends."

"Like who?" Alex teased.

"Vice Principal Clements, Earl the crossing guard, my biology teacher, and all the ladies in the front office," Justin replied smugly.

Alex straightened her cute, red-flowered hoodie and smiled knowingly. "So basically all your friends are adults."

"Yeah, well I fit in best with adults. I'm very mature." Justin liked the sound of that. Maybe it would remind Alex that he was two years older than she was. Maybe she would respect him more.

Suddenly, a loud voice came through the hallway intercom. *"Will Justin Russo report to Lost and Found? We have your cape and light saber."*

Several kids near them stopped talking and stared at Justin and Alex. Alex turned beet red.

"Hmm." Justin shut his locker and marched past Alex to the office to get his stuff. Maybe he'd get the secretaries there to sign his light saber. *That* would show Alex.

Alex rolled her eyes. "I can't believe they found where I hid those," she muttered, heading for the main doors. It was time to leave. No more school for her. Even better, no more being embarrassed by Justin in school. At least for another two months.